The Wizard's Wish

by Damian Harvey

Illustrated by Andy Elkerton

W

FRANKLIN WATTS

LONDON • SYDNEY

First published in 2009 by
Franklin Watts
338 Euston Road
London
NW1 3BH

Franklin Watts Australia
Level 17/207 Kent Street
Sydney
NSW 2000

Text © Damian Harvey 2009
Illustration © Andy Elkerton 2009

A CIP catalogue record for this book is available
from the British Library.

ISBN 978 0 7496 9184 4 (hbk)
ISBN 978 0 7496 9190 5 (pbk)

Series Editor: Jackie Hamley
Editor: Melanie Palmer
Series Advisor: Dr Barrie Wade
Series Designer: Peter Scoulding

Printed in China

Franklin Watts is a division of
Hachette Children's Books,
an Hachette UK company.
www.hachette.co.uk

Marvo's head was
smooth and shiny.

The whiskers on his chin
were short and tiny.

So he gave his wand
a wave in the air ...

… and started to sprout
the most wondrous hair.

He combed it.

He styled it.

6

He made it just right.

But early next morning
he had a big fright.

The hair was still growing.
It was down to the floor!

His beard was curling
out through the door.

It dropped in his soup.

WIZ SPORT

It flopped on his face.

His pesky hair flew
all over the place.

A family of birds made
a nest on his head.

They kept him awake
as he lay in his bed.

"Stop!" he cried.
"I've had quite enough!

24

I wish to be rid of this troublesome fluff."

25

So with a wave of his
wand, the hair was gone.

Now when he goes out,
Marvo puts a hat on.

BEST
WIZARD'S
HATS

28

Puzzle 1

Put these pictures in the correct order.
Now retell the story in your own words.
Is there a lesson in the story?

Puzzle 2

style	hair
care	there

shock	fright
bright	sunlight

star	far
spell	bizarre

Find the non-rhyming word in each word box. Can you think of some words to rhyme with the odd one out?

Answers

Puzzle 1

The correct order is: 1d, 2f, 3a, 4e, 5c, 6b

Puzzle 2

The odd words out are:

style, shock, spell.

Look out for more Leapfrog Rhyme Time:

*hardback

For more Leapfrog books go to: www.franklinwatts.co.uk